Little Rabbit Runaway

HARRY HORSE

For Mandy

PUFFIN BOOKS

Published by the Penguin Group: London, New York, Ireland, Australia, Canada, India, New Zealand and South Africa
Penguin Books Ltd, Registered Offices: 80 Strand, London WC2R 0RL, England

www.penguin.com

First published 2005
Published in this edition 2006
1 3 5 7 9 10 8 6 4 2
Text and illustrations copyright © Harry Horse, 2005
All rights reserved
The moral right of the author/ illustrator has been asserted
Manufactured in China

ISBN-13: 978–0–140–56958–2
ISBN-10: 0–140–56958–8

One day, when he was naughty,
Mama and Papa told Little Rabbit off.

"It's not fair!" cried Little Rabbit.

"Everybody is always telling me off," he said.

"I shall run away and live all by myself."

He packed a few things
for the journey.

"Don't go, Little Rabbit," said Mama.
"We will miss you!"
  "Farewell," said Little Rabbit,
and off he ran.

Little Rabbit ran far away.
Mama and Papa called after him.

He hid under a hedge.

"I shall build a house and stay here forever. I'm Little Rabbit Runaway. Nobody can tell me what to do!"

Little Rabbit had just started building
when along came Molly Mouse.
  "What are you doing?" she said.

"I'm making my very own house,"
said Little Rabbit.
  Molly Mouse asked if she could help.

Little Rabbit said she could, as long as
she did not get in the way.

"We will need more things," said Little Rabbit,
looking around.

Molly Mouse knew just where to find
everything they would need.

Little Rabbit and Molly Mouse carried back
as much as they could.

They built the house together.

When they had finished,
Molly Mouse asked,
"Who's going to live
in this lovely house?"

"I am," said Little Rabbit. "It's mine! I'm Little Rabbit Runaway and nobody can tell me what to do!"

"I ran away too," said Molly Mouse.
"I don't have anywhere to live."

"I know!" said Little Rabbit,
"you could live with me."

So she did.
"Home sweet home,"
said Molly Mouse.

The new house was very comfortable inside.
  "I'll be Mama," said Molly Mouse as she laid
the table and poured the tea.

"No, Little Rabbit, don't sit there.
Sit here!" said Molly Mouse.
"And sit up straight."

She made them a
special acorn cake.

She nibbled the cake into pieces.
"Make sure you eat it all
up," said Molly Mouse.

Little Rabbit did not like Molly Mouse's cake.
"Yuck!" He spat it out. "I only like
my mama's carrot cake."

"What a naughty little rabbit you are," scolded Molly Mouse.
"No, I'm not!" said Little Rabbit. "You're not my real mama
and it's not your house. You can't tell me what to do!"

He got up and ran out the door.

"I'm Little Rabbit Runaway and I do what I want to!" he said.
And so he did.

Little Rabbit rolled in the mud with bull frogs.

He jumped out on some ducklings and scared them.

"Boo!"

And he played in a thorn bush
with a hedgehog.

Soon Little Rabbit was very dirty indeed.

His blue suit was torn.

Then it started to rain.

Little Rabbit ran back to his new house.

"Quick, Molly Mouse. Let me in!" shouted Little Rabbit.

"Careful! You'll knock the whole house down," said Molly Mouse.

"I don't care!" he said. "It's my house! Let me in, you bossyboots!"

Molly Mouse let Little Rabbit
back in.
  "Mind your paws on
the furniture," she said.

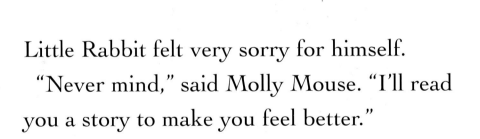

Little Rabbit felt very sorry for himself.
  "Never mind," said Molly Mouse. "I'll read
you a story to make you feel better."

Molly Mouse told Little Rabbit a story about a huge cat that chased after little rabbits who ran away from their mamas.

Little Rabbit got scared.

Molly Mouse got scared too
and jumped into bed beside him.

"What's that noise?" whispered Molly Mouse.

"Is it the cat?" Little Rabbit whispered back.

Then came a thumping on the door.

BANG!

BANG!

BANG!

"It *is* the cat!" squeaked Molly Mouse.

"Come to eat us up!" wailed Little Rabbit.

"I'll never run away from Mama again," he sobbed.

The door opened . . .

. . . Little Rabbit leaped out of bed.

"It's Mama!" cried Little Rabbit. He ran and hugged his mama.
"And my mummy too!" said Molly Mouse.

Little Rabbit had liked living in his own house but he was very pleased to see Mama. So Little Rabbit said goodbye to Molly Mouse and then Mama took him home.

Later, after his bath...

and lots of hugs...

Little Rabbit told everyone all about his day
with Molly Mouse and his very own house.

When he was snuggled up in his real bed, Little Rabbit said,
"I'm not Little Rabbit Runaway any more, Mama.
I'm just your Little Rabbit."

Mama said that she was glad.

"Besides, one mama is enough for me," added Little Rabbit.
"That Molly Mouse is a real bossyboots."